To Terry
A Good Bear Friend
Very Best Wishes

Alexandra Kurland

Edgrr
The Bear Who Wanted To Be Real

written by
Alexandra Kurland

with drawings by
Mark Kenyon

A Kenyon Bear Book

Bear Hollow Press   Delmar   New York

For Real Bears
and all those whose good thoughts
help to keep them in this world.

Copyright © 1987 by Alexandra Kurland
All rights reserved
No part of this book may be reproduced in any form or by any means,
except for the inclusion of brief quotations in a review,
without permission in writing from the publisher.
Requests for permission to make copies of any part of the work
should be mailed to:
Permissions, Bear Hollow Press
110 Salisbury Road
Delmar, New York 12054
Printed in the United States of America
Library of Congress Cataloging in Publication Data
Kurland, Alexandra. Edgrr,
the bear who wanted to be real.
(A Kenyon Bear book)
Summary: While picnicking in the woods with the
other teddy bears, Edgrr tries to prove that he is
a real bear.
[1. Teddy bears – Fiction] I. Kenyon, Mark, ill.
II. Title. III. Series: Kurland, Alexandra. Kenyon Bear book.
PZ7.K958Ed 1987 [Fic] 87-19339
ISBN 0-938209-36-1
ISBN 0-938209-45-0

Table Of Contents

Chapter		
	INTRODUCTION	5
One	EDGRR AND THE REAL BEARS	6
Two	WHATEVER CAN WE DO?	9
Three	KENYON VENTURES OUT	14
Four	SNOW DAY	18
Five	GHOST STORY	27
Six	EDGRR IN THE DARK WOODS	32
Seven	RACCOON ADVENTURE	39
Eight	THE JOURNEY HOME	48
	AFTERWORD	53

INTRODUCTION

I am so glad you came to visit today! Kenyon Bear stopped by this morning.

You remember Kenyon. I told you about him in **Teddies To The Rescue**. He's my friend who lives in the Shuttle Hill Herb Shop. You must have seen him all dressed up in the window as Santa Bear, or the Easter Bunny.

I haven't seen Kenyon for a long time. The last time he came to visit he had the most awful head cold. He sounded all stuffed up. I joked that teddy bears should be used to being stuffed, but he didn't think that was very funny.

He just kept grumbling about a bear named Edgrr. I remember I sat him down in the best chair by the fire and fixed him a mug of steaming hot cocoa.

I was hoping he'd tell me a story, and I wasn't disappointed. Kenyon is the best story teller I know. He told me all about Edgrr, and I can see why he's cross with him, even though the story does have a happy ending. But I better start at the beginning, or you'll get confused.

CHAPTER ONE
Edgrr And The Real Bears

Edgrr was a teddy bear. He lived in the window of the Herb Shop along with all the other bears. The problem was that Edgrr did not want to be a teddy bear. He did not want to be cute or cuddly. He did not want to be picked up and hugged. When people came to the Herb Shop to buy a teddy bear Edgrr would look fierce. If they picked him up, he would scowl at them.

"I don't like this bear," they would say. "He's too cross. I want one that's smiling and happy." Then they would drop him and choose another bear, and Edgrr would be pleased.

Kenyon Bear did not understand. Kenyon was the shop's bear. He was bigger than the others, and he lived in the window year round.

Kenyon liked to help the little bears find good homes. He didn't mind not being adopted himself. The shop was his home, and he had many good friends who came to visit. But he did *not* understand Edgrr.

Just before opening every morning Kenyon did a check of the window. It was his job to make sure all the bears were back in their places before any people came in. After a full night of playing it wasn't always easy to remember where everyone belonged.

On this particular morning Kenyon looked around at each of his friends. Chester was sitting up straight and tall on Hector the toy horse. Six little bears were sledding down a hill of cotton snow. In the side window four more bears were cutting out Valentines.

"One, two, three, four . . ." Kenyon did his head count. "Wait a minute, I'm missing someone. Oh no, where's Edgrr?"

Kenyon checked the window again, but Edgrr was not to be seen. The shop would be open any moment. He couldn't start a search now. They'd be caught.

And then he saw Edgrr. He was hiding behind a table over by the tea cupboard. But it was too late to do anything about it. The key turned in the latch, and the shop owners walked in.

"Get over here at once," Kenyon hissed. "Someone will see you."

"Then I shall growl and scare them away," declared Edgrr. "I am a real bear. I won't sit in the window anymore. I won't! I won't! I won't! And you can't make me." He ducked under the table cover and hid between two large cartons.

Kenyon groaned, but he couldn't move from the window. A young mother came in with her two little girls. They came up to the front of the shop to pick out a bear. Kenyon watched in horror as Edgrr crept out from under the table and stalked up behind the little girls. He was growling under his breath and looking his very fiercest.

The eldest girl turned around and saw him, but she wasn't a bit afraid. She picked him up and gave him a big hug. Edgrr went limp and put on his scowliest face.

"What about this one, Mommy?" asked the little girl, holding him up so he could be seen.

"No, I don't think so, dear. He doesn't look very happy. Put him back in the window. What about this one? I like this bear."

She picked up a cinnamon colored bear who smiled and grinned, and could barely keep from laughing out loud at the thought of being adopted. The little girls liked him too, so the shop owners tucked him away in a pretty bear bag and off he went to his new home.

CHAPTER TWO
Whatever Shall We Do?

All day long Edgrr lay in a heap just as the little girl had left him. Kenyon shook his head. He just did not understand him.

"Don't you want to be adopted?" he asked. "Don't you want to be loved?"

"No," Edgrr growled. "Real bears do not need love. Real bears live in a woods and eat berries. Real bears do not need anybody."

Kenyon sighed, but it made him sad to think of all the wonderful things Edgrr was missing.

"We must help him," Kenyon said to the other bears. The shop was closed for the night, and all the people had gone home to their nice warm houses.

"We must show him what it is like to be loved."

"But how?" asked all the other bears.

"I do not know," Kenyon sighed, "but we must think of something. We must."

So all the bears sat and thought. Kenyon wrinkled up his forehead as hard as he could. No one said anything. The shop got very very quiet. Outside the wind howled and blew up gusts of snow against the window. It was a cold February night and Kenyon was glad to be inside.

"That's it!" he exclaimed.

"What's it? What is it?"

But Kenyon put his paw to his lips and winked meaningfully in Edgrr's direction. "Shh.... I'll tell you later."

And later he did just that. In whispered tones he told the bears his plan. If Edgrr thought being a real bear was so great, well, they'd just show him what it was really like. On Sunday when the shop was closed, they would take him out in the woods behind the shop.

"All of us?" protested one little bear. "But it's cold."

"And it's snowy," said another.

"Well, maybe we could have a campfire," said Kenyon, "but just a little one for us."

"Could we roast marshmallows?" piped up another bear.

"And tell ghost stories..." said another.

"And go sledding..."

"And skiing..."

Well, before they knew it, the bears had completely forgotten that the whole idea was to teach Edgrr a lesson, and had planned instead the most glorious holiday.

Finding sleds and skis was no problem. The bears had those to play with in the window. But there was not a marshmallow nor a drop of cocoa to be had in the shop.

"I shall have to go to the grocery store," Kenyon said very importantly.

It was a place he had heard the shop's owners talk about many times, but he had never been. Before opening early on Saturday morning, he climbed down out of the window and went to the back, to the change drawer, and took out a few dollars. Then he pulled out the box where he kept all his hats and other props for the window. He had quite a collection—a sailor's cap, a Santa Claus hat, a London bobby's helmet, even a long pair of rabbit ears for Easter

But none of them seemed quite right for wearing to the *Grocery Store*. But then what did a well-dressed bear wear to the grocery store?

Kenyon wasn't really sure. He tried on a straw boater and looked at himself in the mirror. He looked quite dapper. All he needed were white spats and a cane. But he didn't think that it was somehow quite right. He didn't want people to stare.

Probably, if grocery stores were anything like the shop, people wore winter parkas and warm woolen hats. And that's when he remembered that it was cold outside and he had a long walk. So he pulled on his heavy winter boots – the same ones he wore when he shovelled the front walk for the shop's owners – put on his hat, added a long wool scarf, and a parka, and considered himself ready for anything.

He knew the way to the grocery store. He could see the sign from the shop window. But getting there was no easy matter. Nobody bothered to shovel the sidewalks. The snowplows piled the snow up in great drifts and that's where it stayed.

Kenyon grumbled and growled as he struggled along. He kept breaking through the crust. He could feel the snow falling down into his boots and getting his fur wet. Twice he dropped his money and had to hunt for it in the snow. He was glad when he came to driveways and had only the slush to walk through.

He had to cross the street to get to the grocery store. It was a very wide street and even at this early hour the cars were whizzing past in great numbers. Kenyon waited and waited for the road to clear. But each time, just as he thought it was safe to cross, a car would turn in from a sidestreet and come racing past.

"That's not fair! That's not fair," Kenyon growled. "It's my turn. Stop at once!"

And do you know, that is exactly what happened. Each and every one of those cars came to a halt. Kenyon was never so surprised in all of his life. He felt very important. He straightened his hat, brushed the snow off his coat and started across.

Of course, if he had bothered to look up he would have seen the red traffic light. But Kenyon didn't know about lights. All he knew was that the cars had stopped for him. He strolled across, bowing his head slightly now and then, and giving a slight wave of his paw. A few of the drivers stared, but most of them were too busy watching the light to notice. And the ones that did notice a large teddy bear walking across the street didn't think much of it. After all, it was early in the morning and anything can happen before your second cup of coffee.

Kenyon gave a final salute with his paw and stepped to the curb. And just as he did, the light turned green and the cars rushed forward.

"Hey! Well I never!" said Kenyon. "How rude." But then he forgot all about it because he had reached the **Grocery Store** and a whole new adventure.

CHAPTER THREE
Kenyon Ventures Out

Kenyon walked up to the door marked:

ENTRANCE

It was a big heavy door. He was wondering how on earth he was going to open it when – whoosh – it opened all by itself.

Kenyon wasn't too sure he trusted doors that did that. Such a door might just as easily whoosh shut just as a teddy bear was walking through. He put his paw against the glass panels and edged his way in. He was two steps clear and – snick – it closed tight.

It made him jump, but he quickly forgot about doors. He was too busy staring to worry about anything but what was in front of him.

The grocery store was huge, and filled with colour and light and the most wonderful smells. He didn't know where to look first, but his bear's nose could definitely smell honey. And right in front of him was a big bin of nuts: walnuts and peanuts and . . . but no. He had come for marshmallows. Marshmallows for a cookout, and maybe some honey, but first he had to find the marshmallows. So he started up one aisle and down the next.

No one paid any attention to the small figure bundled up in boots, parka, and a thick hat. Kenyon certainly didn't bother with them. He was too busy looking at the shelves of soups, and cake mixes, and cookies. Cookies would be good on a cookout. He took down a bag of honey covered graham crackers and another of chocolate chips.

In the household section he found a long box of wooden safety matches. With the teas and coffee he found cocoa.

At the bakery he ordered a dozen sticky buns (for the bears who didn't like cookies.) The lady behind the counter stared long and hard at him, but she handed over a large bag filled with buns.

He finally found the marshmallows in the candy section. He picked up a bag and then thought again. One bag certainly wasn't enough, not for teddy bears. But was two going to do it? He poked the marshmallows and weighed the bag in his paws. No certainly not, he needed four bags and not a marshmallow less.

He balanced his parcels in his paw and headed for the checkout counter. But he had to stop first at the honey. No cookout would be complete without honey, and here were three large jugs filled with the most sweet smelling honey.

"May I help you?" A clerk had come up and was hovering at his shoulder.

"Oh yes, please. I'd like one of each," said Kenyon.

"One of each," said the clerk doubtfully, but she poured out from the big jugs three little jars of honey.

And now Kenyon took his armful of cocoa, and cookies, and sticky buns, and matches, and four bags of marshmallows, and three jars of honey, and went up to the front of the store. Luckily, there wasn't much of a line. His things tumbled out of his paws onto the counter.

The check-out clerk started adding them up without even looking at Kenyon.

"That'll be $12.81," she said

"Oh, dear," said Kenyon, "Oh dear. I don't have that much."

The clerk stared at him and then stared again. "Is this some kind of a joke?"

"No! I'm sorry. I'm afraid I got rather carried away." And he looked sadly at the counter.

"Well, you'll have to put some of it back. How much do you have?"

Kenyon counted out his change. "Seven dollars and thirty five cents. I suppose, I suppose I don't really need the cookies . . . ."

"Or all these marshmallows."

"But I came especially for those," said Kenyon in distress. "I couldn't put those back. No, everything else but the marshmallows."

"Well . . ." began the clerk, and then she melted. Nobody can resist teddy bear eyes for very long. Kenyon bought his marshmallows, and his matches, and cocoa, and one little jar of honey, and the clerk didn't mind when he was ten cents short. She packed up his things in a large paper bag and, when Kenyon wasn't looking, slipped in a bag of cookies besides.

Kenyon thanked her very much and was off. The door whooshed open and snicked closed just as before. But he didn't mind. He was feeling quite pleased with himself, even though he had had to leave so many lovely treats behind.

The cars stopped for him, too, just as before, and he was soon home telling the other bears about his wonderful adventure. He hid the groceries away in the bottom of his costume trunk, and hopped back into the window just as the shop was opening up for the day.

CHAPTER FOUR
Snow Day

The next day was Sunday, and the shop was closed. All the bears were very excited about their holiday, and especially Edgrr. He could hardly wait to get started, but Kenyon took his time packing.

"We don't want to forget anything," he said firmly.

He found a knapsack and a pair of binoculars in his box of props. He carefully packed the marshmallows – all four bags, the matches, a book on bird watching, and two or three other odds and ends that 'might come in handy.'

The little bears took their skis and sleds out of the window, and then at last they were all ready to go.

Edgrr led the way into the woods. The weather was warmer than it had been for Kenyon's shopping trip. The bears were quite comfortable with only their fur coats to protect them. And Edgrr flatly refused to wear a hat. Real bears did not wear hats. (Though many of the little bears had worn theirs and before the day was out they were very glad they had.)

Edgrr found a path that took them through a dark stand of spruce trees. It was very still and quiet under their branches, but the sun was shinning and none of the bears felt afraid.

The path brought them to the edge of a hill just right for sledding. They could play here all day with the trees to their backs and the open fields and hills before them.

The bears wasted no time getting out their skis and sleds. Kenyon helped them tie up their laces, and then they were off – shwoosh, whoosh across the snow. Or rather flop, plop into the snow. The teddy bears soon learned that dreaming about skiing and actually doing it were two very different things. They found it wasn't easy standing up even when they weren't moving.

And when they tried to move, well that was a disaster. More than one teddy bear ended up on his backside with his skis in the air.

But what was worse was to just get your balance, to have everything going just right, and then to have another teddy get in your way.

SNOW DAY

The teddy bears decided that maybe, just maybe they weren't meant to be skiers. But sledding, that was another matter. Anyone could go sledding. So the bears went whooshing down the hill on their little wooden sleds. They took turns hauling the sleds up. That was the hard part, but it was worth it. They had never known anything so exciting in all their lives.

And then Edgrr discovered that you didn't need a sled at all. He belly flopped down on the snow and slid all the way to the bottom of the hill. Soon all the bears joined him, and they didn't even notice how cold and wet their tummies were getting. All the bears joined in, that is all except for one, Kenyon. He sat at the top of the hill and enjoyed the others' fun, but he wasn't about to go tumbling down that hill. He was too old and too big for that.

But he was not to be left in peace. A cubby bear noticed him sitting by himself.

"Come on, Kenyon," he called, "come slide down."

And then all the bears joined in. They scrambled up to the top of the hill and pulled him to his feet.

"You have to try it, just once. Come on, Kenyon. You'll love it."

"No. I'm too old. I don't want to. Don't push. Oh, all right, all right. Only don't push."

Kenyon lowered himself very slowly onto his stomach.

"Stay back, all of you. I'm going, only don't hurry me. No, I don't need a push."

He looked down over the slope. From this angle the hill looked even steeper and longer than he had imagined possible.

"I shall break my neck," he thought to himself, and then he remembered teddy bears do not have bones to break. He gave himself the gentlest of gentle pushes. He went two inches.

"Harder! Push Harder!" shouted all his friends.

He tried again and felt himself sliding, slowly. The hill rolled gently out from under him and then dropped off sharply. And suddenly he was picking up speed. He was whirling away, out of control down the hill. He was rolling and tumbling . . . . He was spinning and flying . . . . He was – thump! stopped short in a soft snow drift at the foot of the hill.

Kenyon picked himself up. "Why that was, that was . . . . That was fun!" he exclaimed. "Here, let me do that again." And he bounded up to the top of the hill while the other bears cheered him on.

This time they all rolled down the hill together, everyone except for Edgrr. He stayed at the top and threw snowballs at them.

"Let's get him! Let's get him!" Kenyon cried, but Edgrr had the advantage of the hill.

"Get Kenyon! Get Kenyon!" he shouted back. And that's what everyone did.

"Enough," cried Kenyon, throwing up his paws against a barrage of snowballs. "Uncle, Uncle!" And he fell laughing in the snow with the other teddies tumbling on top of him.

"I'm starving," he declared. "Let's roast some marshmallows." And that's what they did.

They had no trouble finding dry wood for the fire. They gathered up enough for a big bonfire, and each bear saved a long stick for roasting marshmallows.

Kenyon snatched the matches out of a cubby bear's paws. "Don't play with those," he snapped. "We want a campfire not a forest fire. I'll handle the matches. The rest of you stand back."

Lighting the fire was no easy task. Kenyon was afraid of matches. He wouldn't have told a soul, but he was afraid they would flare up and singe his fur. So he held the matches very gingerly between his paws and struck the box ever so gently. Of course, they didn't light. And his paws weren't really made for holding matches. He kept breaking them, and dropping them in the snow.

"Oh dear, oh dear, what's wrong with these things? I shall need two boxes before I'm done."

The other teddies got very quiet. They were counting on having a big bonfire. Their holiday wouldn't be complete if they couldn't roast marshmallows.

Kenyon struggled with match after match, until he had ruined almost the entire box. Finally he got one to light. But that was only the first step. The next was getting the wood to catch fire. The bears had put some dried weeds and leaves under the wood. Kenyon touched the match to that. The fire flared up and then fizzled out.

They rearranged the wood, added more leaves and tried again. This time all the bears got down on their tummies and blew as hard as they could. The fire flickered feebly for a moment and then flared up in a lovely warm glow.

And now was a time to warm cold paws, dry wet fur, and munch marshmallows. Edgrr decided that marshmallows were something real bears ate a lot of. But he couldn't decide how he liked his done best. He tried roasting them slowly so that they were an even crusty brown all around the outside. That was delicious. Then he tried putting them in the hot part of the fire until they burst into flame. They turned black, but inside they were soft and gooey. He liked that, too. It was a hard choice.

"Let's have a ghost story," piped up one of the little bears.

"Yes, Kenyon," said another, "tell us a story."

Kenyon paused in the act of skewering a marshmallow onto his stick.

"I don't know any stories," he teased.

"Of course you do. Tell us a story. Go on, you're the oldest."

"Oh, all right." He thought for a moment, and he stared across the fire right at Edgrr. "All right. Here goes."

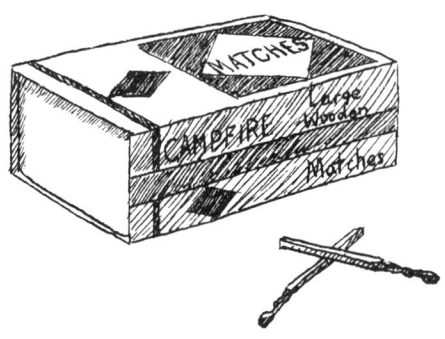

CHAPTER FIVE
Ghost Story

"This is a story about a bear named Rufus. Now Rufus belonged to a little boy who loved him very much. He used to play with him whenever he could, and he took him to bed with him, which Rufus liked very much. But during the day when the little boy was at school, Rufus lived up on the playroom shelf with all the other toys.

He used to get very bored sitting there day after day with nothing to do. He'd look out the window and watch the squirrels playing in the trees, or the dog burying bones in the backyard.

"It must be wonderful to be so free," he thought. "If ever I have the chance I shall run away and be just like them."

Well, one day he got his chance. The little boy took him out in the backyard to play. He put him down under a tree while he built a fort out of sticks to fight off wild Indians. He got so excited about his game that he forgot all about his teddy.

Rufus sat for a long time thinking about the squirrels, and rabbits and other wild things. Then he got up and crept very slowly under the trees and away into the woods. Nobody saw him go, and in a few moments he was running away free as anything.

"This is wonderful!" he cried. "This is just like being a real bear, and I can do anything I please."

And what pleased him was to play all day under the ferns. He tried to get the squirrels to join him, but they only laughed and ran away. So he explored all by himself. He poked about under tree roots and logs. He followed deer trails to see where they went. He paid no attention to where he was going or how long he had been away. Before he knew it, the sun was dipping toward the horizon. It got dark under the trees, and cold. Rufus shivered and wished he were home where it was warm and cozy and people loved him.

GHOST STORY

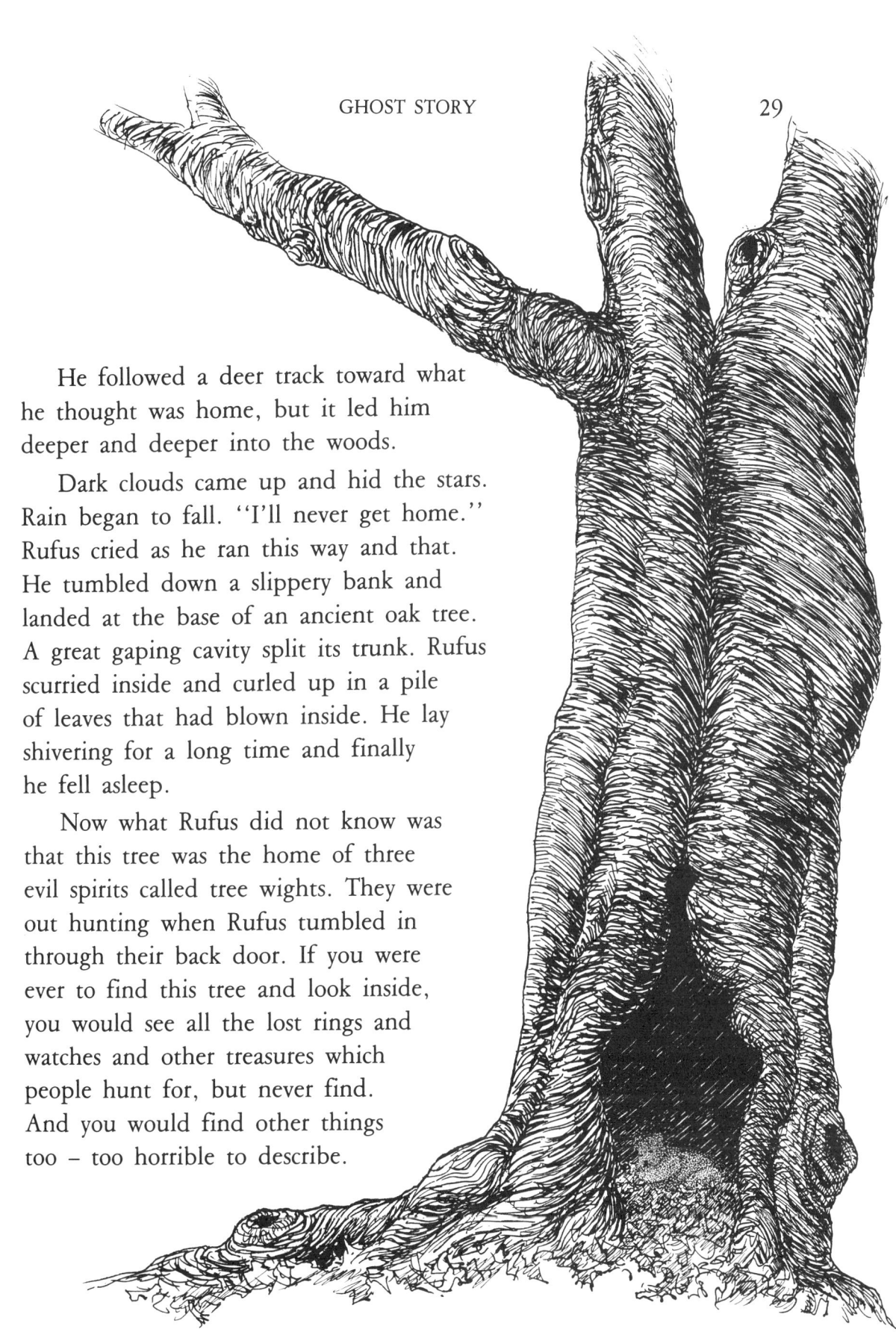

He followed a deer track toward what he thought was home, but it led him deeper and deeper into the woods.

Dark clouds came up and hid the stars. Rain began to fall. "I'll never get home." Rufus cried as he ran this way and that. He tumbled down a slippery bank and landed at the base of an ancient oak tree. A great gaping cavity split its trunk. Rufus scurried inside and curled up in a pile of leaves that had blown inside. He lay shivering for a long time and finally he fell asleep.

Now what Rufus did not know was that this tree was the home of three evil spirits called tree wights. They were out hunting when Rufus tumbled in through their back door. If you were ever to find this tree and look inside, you would see all the lost rings and watches and other treasures which people hunt for, but never find. And you would find other things too – too horrible to describe.

The tree wights returned just before dawn when Rufus was still sound, sound asleep. He was dreaming an odd sort of dream. Something was whispering and muttering. He felt a tree root poking in his side. He stirred and rolled over. But he felt it again, and suddenly he realized that he wasn't asleep and the whispering was all around him.

"Hey!" said a high squeaky voice. "What is it? What's it after?"

"It's after our treasure, it is," said another. "It's come to rob us, it has. To takes all our pretty treasures."

"Aye," said a third. "We must kill it we must. Truss it up and dump it in the river. That's what I say."

Rufus felt something poking him in the side. It felt like a long skinny finger, but he could see nothing.

"It's fat," said the first voice. "We'll roast it, and boil it, and eats it, we will."

"No!" Rufus cried, springing to his feet. "No, leave me alone." He felt hands grabbing him, holding him. He kicked as hard as he could, and the hands let go. He ran from the tree. He ran as hard and as fast as he could, and he never dared to look back.

But the tree wights could not follow. Night was their only time, and the dawn saved him. The first lines of crimson were showing through the night sky or he would never have escaped alive.

Rufus ran until he could run no more. Then he collapsed in a fern bank. He was a sad lost, lonely little teddy bear. He lay for a long long time. I think he slept for a while, but when he woke he heard a voice, not the high awful voice of the tree wights, but a soft voice calling his name. He sat up and listened. It was his own little boy looking for him. Rufus ran to meet him, and I can't say which of the two was the happier to see the other. They went home hand in paw, and Rufus never again strayed away.

CHAPTER SIX
Edgrr In The Dark Woods

Kenyon finished his story and looked round at the circle of frightened little bears. He told a good ghost story.

"Brr," said one. "Do you suppose the trees really are haunted? I should hate to be out after dark."

"So should I," said another. "Its awfully cold, and the fire's almost out. Shouldn't we be going home?"

"That's silly" said Edgrr, puffing out his chest. "I'm not afraid of the dark, or any wood spirits. Real bears aren't afraid of anything."

"That's all very well," said Kenyon, "but it is getting dark, and I for one shall be glad to be inside. Come on. Let's tidy up and go home."

The bears gathered up all their things, but Edgrr refused to move.

"I'm not going back. I don't want to be a teddy bear. I'm going to be a real bear and live in the woods."

Kenyon didn't argue. He motioned to the others. They picked up their sleds, their skis, their empty marshmallow bags, and left. Edgrr sat with his back to them. The teddy bear in him wanted to get up and run after them, but he couldn't. Not after all he had said.

The woods were very still, very quiet, and suddenly very dark. The sun goes down fast in the winter. The trees seemed taller. They leaned out over his head, spreading their dark branches over him. Edgrr shivered and crept closer to the fire.

"Real bears don't use fire. They live in caves or under trees." And then he thought of Rufus and the tree wights. He threw another stick on the fire, and he tried not to think how hungry he was getting. Marshmallows do not fill a teddy bear up for very long.

A little voice inside him kept saying – *"I want to go home. I don't want to be here. I want to go home and be with the others."*

Edgrr shook himself. He wouldn't listen. He was a real bear. But he was hungry, and it was cold.

A long way off a dog barked and another answered. Edgrr shivered. What if they found him and decided he was good to eat.

"I want to go home," said the little voice.

"I am a real bear," said Edgrr.

And as he sat shivering and feeling sorry for himself, it started to snow. At first it was just a few soft flakes floating down. But they were joined by others falling fast and heavy. The snow piled up around him. It put out the last of the fire. Poor Edgrr, he crept back under the trees, shaking the heavy snow from his coat.

"I want to go home," said the voice.

"I am a real bear," said Edgrr. "real bears do not mind the snow. They sleep away the winter in nice cozy caves."

He stomped his paws and ran deeper into the woods. Under the spruce trees the snow was not so heavy. He took refuge under their branches, while the snow fell softly around him.

"I won't go home, I won't," he whispered. "I am a real bear."

But Edgrr wasn't the only one to find shelter in the spruce tree. A dark shadow lighted in the branches above him and let out a mournful cry.

Edgrr froze. "Tree wights!"

The cry came again. Edgrr sprang from his hiding place and raced madly away. The movement silenced the screech owl roosting above him. It swept out on silent wings and disappeared into the night.

Edgrr fled up the path, only now it was hard to follow. Did it turn right or left? Did it go up hill or down? He didn't remember this big log, or all these brambles catching at his fur. He pushed his way through. Surely this stream hadn't been here, and they hadn't walked nearly this far. He was lost.

"I want to go home," shouted the little voice, and this time Edgrr had no answer.

He turned and retraced his steps as best he could, but the snow was drifting and blowing up over the tracks.

He struggled through the drifts, turning first this way and then that. But always he seemed to be going deeper and deeper into the woods.

Suddenly he froze. Something was breaking and crashing through the underbrush. He tried to hide under a fallen tree limb.

"Its tree wights. I know it is," he whispered. "they've come to catch me and eat me. Oh, I want to go home."

But it wasn't the tree wights. It was a dog, a large bouncy, brown spaniel with floppy ears and a wet shaggy coat. She came crashing through the underbrush and sniffed her way right to Edgrr's hiding place.

"So that's what you are! A teddy bear! I sniffed you and sniffed you, but I couldn't guess what you were. Such a funny smell – soggy teddy bear!"

But Edgrr wasn't listening. "Don't eat me! Don't eat me!" He pleaded.

"Eat you! Don't be silly. I've better things to put in my mouth than wet teddy bears. What on earth are you doing here?"

"I . . . I live here," said Edgrr trying to sound very brave and bearlike.

"Live here! Well, its a very silly place to live, if you ask me. I wouldn't have it for tuppence. I've a nice warm fire waiting for me. What do you mean *live here*?"

Edgrr was about to answer, but the dog interrupted.

"There, did you hear that?"

Edgrr stopped to listen. From not far off he heard someone calling.

"Tabitha, c'mon girl. Here, Tabby. C'mon Tabby."

"So sorry," said the dog. "Would love to stay and chat, but I must run. That's for me, and I don't intend to get left out on a night like this."

The dog ran back the way she had come. Edgrr felt even more sorry for himself then before. He crawled out from under the tree limb and followed Tabitha's tracks.

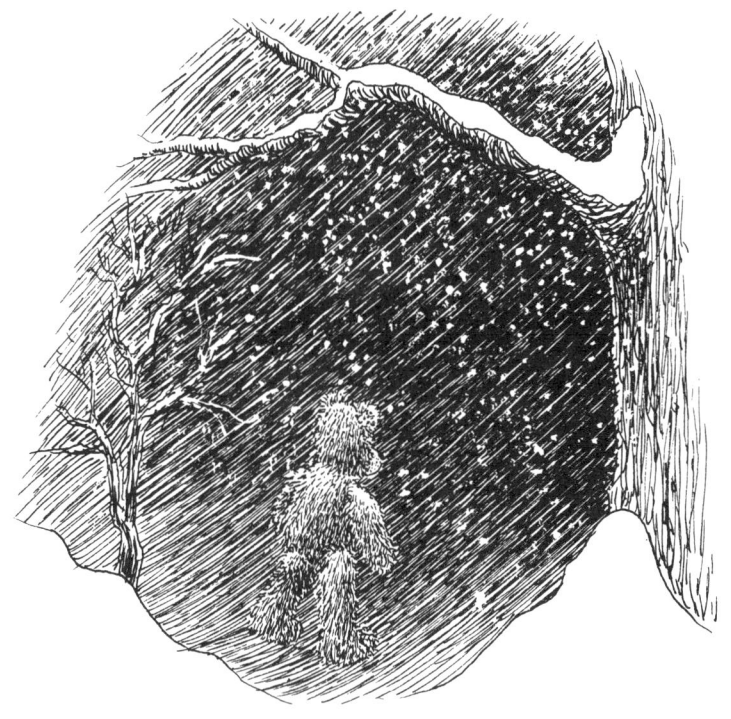

CHAPTER SEVEN
Raccoon Adventure

Edgrr tried to run after Tabitha, but the snow was too deep. He tripped and fell forward, hitting his head hard against a tree root. For a long time he did not stir. Ever so slowly he started to feel again. He felt his frozen, cold paws, and his wet, soggy fur. And he felt something else. Something, or rather, someone, was poking and prodding him in his side.

His teddy bear heart jumped. Tree wights! He was too afraid to move. He heard a sniffling and a snuffling, and felt two little hands pulling at his fur.

"What is it, I'm wondering? All stiff and frozen in the snow," said a voice with a thick country accent.

Edgrr didn't know what tree wights sounded like. Ever so slowly he opened his eyes. What he saw was a huge furry creature with a long snout and a black mask over its eyes.

Now Edgrr might have been a frightened little teddy bear inside, but he did the one thing a real bear would do. He growled. It came out more of a gurgle he was so cold. The creature sat back on his haunches and laughed.

"And what d'you think yer doing?" it asked.

"I'm growling," said Edgrr. "I'm a real bear and I'm going to scare you away."

"Oh, are you indeed? Well, I'm a real raccoon, and I'm not afraid. So what d'you think about that?" Edgrr didn't know what to think. He'd heard of raccoons. Kenyon had told him stories about raccoons. But he couldn't remember — were teddy bears something they ate?

The raccoon was still laughing and chuckling to himself.

"A bear, is it?. Well, well. I haven't heard of a bear in these parts since, well, since before owl's time, and he knows all the stories. But if you're a real bear, why aren't you asleep? I thought bears slept all winter."

"No, they don't. And anyway, I woke up. I was tired of sleeping."

"Tired is it? Well, that's the silliest thing I ever did hear. If I could be asleep on a night like this, believe me I would. I wouldn't be about trying to fill my belly on odd bits of roots and grubs, I can tell you. Not a fit night to be out. All this snow makes for slim pickings."

The raccoon started to move off.

"Wait!" Edgrr cried.

The raccoon turned and looked at him.

"For what?" he asked.

"I, um, I, oh never mind." Edgrr sat dejectedly down in the snow. He couldn't think of any reason for him to stay.

"Are you sure you'd be a real bear, now?" the raccoon chuckled. "You look more like a soggy rabbit to me. Never mind. You can tag along if you like. Are you hungry? I'm just off for a bit of supper myself."

"Oh, yes! I'm starved." Edgrr jumped to his feet and followed after the raccoon.

They went along an old stream bed. The snow came almost up to Edgrr's waist. He tried to step exactly in the raccoons pawprints, but he almost had to swim through the deeper drifts.

The raccoon stopped at a rotten tree stump sticking up above the snow. He tore into the wood, sniffing and snuffling through the larger pieces. At its heart he found a thick white grub. His paws worked like fingers to pick it out. Edgrr turned away in disgust and tried not to watch as the raccoon gulped it down.

"Want one?" he asked.

Edgrr shuddered.

"Funny, I thought bears liked grubs and insects."

"No, they don't. Bears eat blackberries and honey."

"Well, then you must go a long time between meals. I have yet to see a blackberry growing in winter. And as for honey, I should like to eat that, too, but I don't know many bees who are willing to share. Oh, well. Never mind, I'll find us something better. Never did care much for grubs myself. Nasty, bitter things really."

The raccoon moved off. He had a funny rolling, ambling sort of a walk. But he stayed above the snow. Edgrr with his big paws sank deep with every step. He had trouble keeping up.

"Wait for me!" he puffed out.

The raccoon looked back and chuckled. "Now I know why bears sleep all winter." But he waited for Edgrr to catch up. They crossed over the dog Tabitha's tracks. He sniffed and snuffled and followed them back towards the houses. Before long Edgrr saw a glow of lights through the trees, and they were standing by a narrow strip of lawn.

The raccoon tested the air, and then walked boldly out into the open. He went straight up to the house.

"What are you doing? Where are you going?" Edgrr cried.

"You'll see," said the raccoon. "We'll have a bit of fun and a good meal besides."

He went round to the front of the house, straight to the garage. The door was slightly ajar. The raccoon pushed it the rest of the way open with his nose. He went right inside, bold as ever you please. Edgrr hesitated at the entrance. It wasn't right to walk into people's houses.

"You can't go in there! It's not right!" he cried.

"Not right, is it? What a silly thing to say. I'm a raccoon. I go where I please. Well, come on, I thought you were hungry. I can use your help with this."

Edgrr crept in. Two cars parked side by side made for a tight squeeze. The lawn mower, a ten speed bike, a rake, and stacks of old newspapers all were shoved to the back. But standing in the middle were two big trash cans full to overflowing.

The raccoon chuckled to himself. "Look at that. They don't even bother to tie the lids down. Getting sloppy, they are. Ah, well, better for me. Stand clear a minute." He stood up on his hind legs and toppled over first one can, then the other. Bags of trash clattered to the floor and scattered their contents under the two cars.

"They almost make it too easy to be fun. Well, come on. Dig in."

Once again Edgrr watched in disgust as the raccoon nosed through empty food cans and greasy tin foils.

"Well, come on, come on. There's plenty here."

"I – I'm not hungry anymore," said Edgrr, and he tried not to think about the empty rumblings in his stomach.

"Not hungry, is it. And with all these good pickings, too. Just what is it you do eat anyway?"

"I eat, I eat marshmallows, and cookies, and cocoa."

"Marshmallows. That I know. They bloom down by the brook in the spring. Can't say I favor 'em much myself. But cookies – cocoa? Never heard of 'em. It's no wonder bears don't live around here anymore. They all starved to death. Now what you want is a good empty soup can and some chicken bones."

The raccoon nosed among the empty food tins. Suddenly, he paused. His ears pricked back and forth, and his nose sniffed the air. "More's the pity it is. Fun time's over."

"Why, what is it?"

"We've been discovered. Better clear out."

A light from the house clicked on, and the back door opened.

"Those darn raccoons," came a man's angry voice. "They've been at the trash again."

The Raccoon scooted out the garage door just as the man stepped out of the house. But Edgrr wasn't quick enough. He huddled out of sight under the car, not sure what to do.

"Come back in," came a woman's voice. "It's too cold outside. We'll clean it up in the morning."

The man slammed the garage door shut and went back inside. Edgrr shivered. Now what was he to do? He'd never get that door open. They'd find him in the morning, a poor frozen teddy bear. He tried stomping up and down to stay warm, but his stuffing was already frozen. So he sat down on a pile of newspapers and let a big tear roll down his teddy bear face.

"I want to go home," came the little voice, and this time Edgrr did not argue. Kenyon and the others would be back in the shop all warm and toasty. Edgrr could see them. They'd have tidied up the shop by now and done all their chores. Kenyon would have one or two of the little bears on his lap and he'd be reading a story.

"I'm a real bear," Edgrr whimpered. "I will curl up under these newspapers and go to sleep, and when I wake up it will be spring." He tried to make a little nest for himself. He tucked his paws under him and tried to think warm spring thoughts.

Suddenly he heard a scritch, scratching at the garage door. "Raccoon? Is that you?" he whispered. "Oh, please be you."

But for answer all he got was a creaking of the door on its hinges. Ever so slowly it opened a crack, and the raccoon poked his long snout round the corner.

"Well, don't just sit there gawking," he said. "They always come back to check. It's part of the game. Better clear out while you can."

Edgrr followed the raccoon out, back along the foundation the way they had come. A light was still on at the back of the house, but the raccoon headed boldly off across the lawn. Edgrr started to follow, but at the edge of the woods he hesitated.

"Well, aren't you coming?" asked the raccoon.

Edgrr shook his head.

"You are the funniest thing I ever did meet. Are you sure you're a real bear?" But Edgrr was already running back towards the house. The raccoon didn't stay to watch. He disappeared like a shadow into the trees.

CHAPTER EIGHT
The Journey Home

Edgrr didn't know what he was going to do, but lights meant people. They meant a roof over his head and a warm fire. They meant drying out and snuggling under blankets with a hot cup of cocoa. They meant being a teddy bear and having a home, and being loved.

For the first time that sounded better than being a real bear. In fact, it sounded exactly like what Edgrr wanted more than anything else in the world. It was all very well for the raccoon. He was made for the woods and the wild life. Edgrr could dream about the deep forest, but he belonged to a different world. He understood that now, and he understood what being a teddy bear really meant.

The back door was closed tight against the night. "Let me in. Let me in," Edgrr cried in his teddy bear voice, but the wind was howling and no one heard.

He went round to the side windows. The owners of the house had put wooden frames over the bushes that grew by the window. Edgrr climbed up on top of them and peered inside. The light was still on. He could clearly see everything in the room.

Tabitha was lying on the hearth, with the warm embers of the fire still glowing warm behind her. The man who had startled the raccoon was tidying up before going to bed. He put the day's newspapers in a pile, straightened the cushions in the sofa. Then he reached down and gave Tabitha a goodnight scratch. She thumped her tail lazily against the floor.

Edgrr banged on the window pane. "Let me in. Let me in," he cried, but still no one heard.

The light clicked off, and he could see nothing. But he knew Tabitha was warm and toasty by the fire, and her owner was going upstairs to bed.

He felt colder than ever. He climbed down off his perch and tried to think clear thoughts, but all he knew was that he was cold and wet and wanted to go home.

A snowplow came clattering down the road and sent a spray of slush up over his head. But it left a clear road behind it. A road that might lead to other warm houses, or even the shop.

Edgrr scrambled up and over the huge snow bank the plow left behind. He dropped down onto the road, but which way to go, right or left?

He looked as far as he could in both directions and finally for no reason at all turned off to the right. The houses were all dark as pitch. Everyone had gone to bed. He thought of going up to each one and banging on the door until somebody heard, until somebody let him in. But the driveways were all choked with snow from the plow.

He stumbled on. He could feel his stuffing starting to freeze. His legs got stiff and he felt sleepy.

"Why doesn't somebody come and get me," he moaned. "Oh, I wish I had a little boy to come and find me."

The houses stood closer together now, and ahead he saw lights! He hurried on. They weren't warm inside lights, but street lights. He came to the head of a big intersection and in front of him was a grocery store. Its big neon lights shone brightly through the snow.

A grocery store . . .

That meant, that meant . . .

Edgrr hardly dared to think.

That meant the shop was just around the corner! — the shop and the bears, and hot cocoa, and a warm dry bed.

He made his legs run as fast as they could. He ran down the road, which was a dangerous thing to do, but the road was empty. Not another soul was stirring on this cold winter night.

He could see the shop now with its sign in the window. The bears were just dark shadows behind the glass.

And now he was banging and knocking and calling to be let in.

Kenyon had waited up for him. The other bears, exhausted from their holiday, were sleeping and dreaming good teddy bear dreams. But Kenyon had Edgrr inside, and wrapped in a warm blanket, and sipping hot cocoa faster than you would think possible.

He didn't say anything about real bears. He knew he didn't have to.

The shop opened late Monday morning because of the snow. All the sleds and skis were back where they belonged. And Edgrr was dry and warm, and looking almost as good as new.

A few customers straggled in, stomping the snow off their boots. And then a lady came in with her little boy.

"We've come to pick out a bear," she said. "a very special bear."

This time Edgrr did not scowl when he was picked up. He looked at the little boy and the little boy looked at him.

"This one, mommy. This is the one I want." he said. He gave Edgrr a big hug, and Edgrr gave him a teddy bear hug back.

AFTERWORD

Kenyon came to visit this morning. His cold is all better. He was looking very smug and pleased with himself. Edgrr had been in the shop the day before. Only his name isn't Edgrr anymore. He's just called Bear. Plain and simple.

He came in with his new little boy, Corin. They go everywhere together. They've built forts in the backyard, and gone biking. Corin was in the shop with his mother to buy presents for his aunt and two cousins. They were going to visit them on a lake.

"And do you know what?" Bear whispered to Kenyon. "I'm going with him. We'll go camping, and hiking. I might even see a real bear! But I don't want to be one anymore. I like things just the way they are."

Kenyon stayed for quite a long visit. I fixed him a big piece of choclate cake, and a mug of cocoa. He sat in his favorite chair, and told me another story. I can't stop thinking about it. It was so sad. It's about a bear named Sara. Poor Sara, nobody wanted her, and she ended up being thrown out in the trash. But I better not start that story now. Next time you come I'll tell it to you.

The beary end

We wish to thank all the people who helped with this book, and especially all the children who kept asking when Edgrr would be ready. We also wish to thank Linda Tellington – Jones, founder of Animal Ambassadors, International. Kenyon Bear has become a story collector for Animal Ambassadors, and we are proud of his work on behalf of all animals.

By The Same Author

TEDDIES TO THE RESCUE

Another Kenyon Bear Book